# When I Visit the Farm

CRYSTAL BESHARA

Lobster Press ™

When I Visit the Farm
Text & Illustrations © 2009 Crystal Beshara

Published by Lobster Press™
1620 Sherbrooke Street West, Suites C & D
Montréal, Québec  H3H 1C9
Tel. (514) 904-1100 · Fax (514) 904-1101
www.lobsterpress.com

Publisher: Alison Fripp
Editor: Meghan Nolan
Editorial Assistant: Susanna Rothschild
Graphic Design & Production: Tammy Desnoyers
Consultant on Font & Cover Design: Sara Gillingham
Color Reproduction: Couvrette/Ottawa

We acknowledge the financial support of the Government of Canada through the Book Publishing Industry Development Program (BPIDP) for our publishing activities.

The Canada Council | Le Conseil des Arts
for the Arts | du Canada

We acknowledge the support of the Canada Council for the Arts for our publishing program.

Library and Archives Canada Cataloguing in Publication

Beshara, Crystal, 1975-
    When I visit the farm / Crystal Beshara.

ISBN 978-1-897550-09-0

    1. Farms--Juvenile fiction.  I. Title.
PS8603.E773W44 2009            jC813'.6            C2008-904588-2

Printed and bound in Seoul, South Korea.

To Stuart and Charlotte
for your constant love
and support.

To Mom and Dad
for life-long inspiration and
memories on *our farm*.

When I visit the farm

I feel as free as a dandelion seed.

I have all the space in the world

to spread my wings ...

I love to feel the cool

clean grass between my toes.

I visit my many animal friends.

The Jersey cow

stretches her neck out to say hello.

I touch a nose soft as velvet.

Warm breath fills my hands.

Sometimes I play follow the leader

with the ducklings.

I pretend to be a mother

to these young goslings.

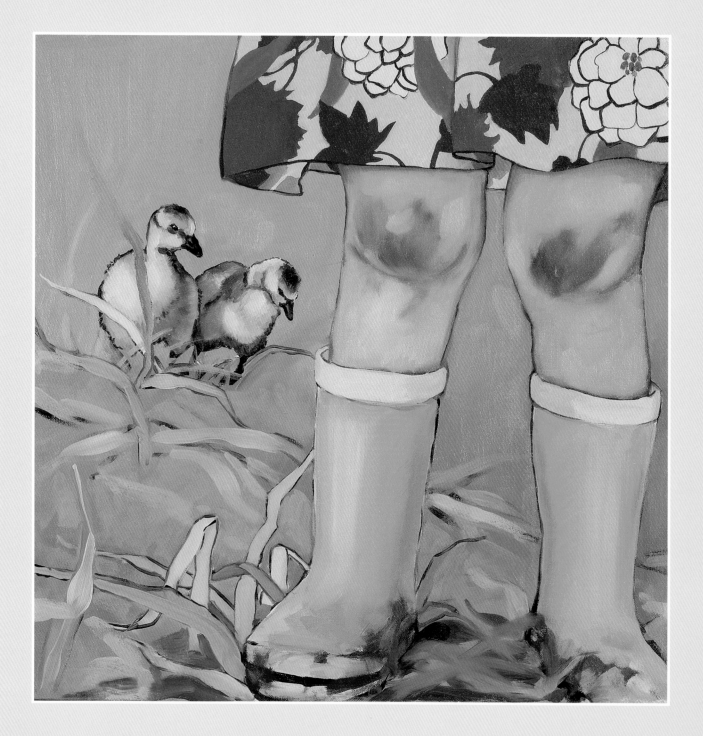

I make the perfect nest
for some tiny golden chicks.

Sometimes I dream that I am drifting as high as the trees.

What would I see?

... my friend

the chipmunk?

... a nest of robin's eggs

as blue as the sky?

I meet a new friend – an old hen

who lives near the barn.

She too has a dream.

To know what it is like to be free.

What is your
dream?